THE PROBLEM WITH PULCIFER

THE PROBLEM WITH PULCIFER

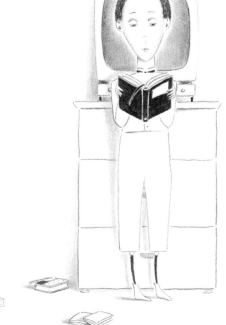

BY *FLORENCE PARRY HEIDE*
PICTURES BY *JUDY GLASSER*

J.B. LIPPINCOTT   NEW YORK

The Problem with Pulcifer
Text copyright © 1982 by Florence Parry Heide
Illustrations copyright © 1982 by Judy Glasser
J.B. Lippincott Junior Books,
10 East 53rd Street,
New York, N. Y. 10022.
Published simultaneously in Canada by
Fitzhenry & Whiteside Limited, Toronto.
Library of Congress Cataloging in Publication Data

Heide, Florence Parry.
The Problem with Pulcifer.

Summary: Pulcifer's preference for books is
considered a grave problem by the television-
addicted world around him.
[1. Television–Fiction.   2. Books and reading–
Fiction]   I. Glasser, Judy, ill.   II. Title.
PZ7.H36Pr 1982   [Fic]   81-48606
ISBN 0-397-32001-9   AACR2
ISBN 0-397-32002-7 (lib. bdg.)

2 3 4 5 6 7 8 9 10

First Edition

With love to Parry and Veronica
and their David

Pulcifer had a problem.

He knew he had a problem because he had heard his parents talking about it. About his p-r-o-b-l-e-m. Actually, that was how he had learned to spell his name. Listening to his parents.

"What on earth are we going to do about P-u-l-c-i-f-e-r?"

Pulcifer's problem was that he didn't watch television.

"You're not really trying, Pulcifer," said Pulcifer's mother.

"When I was your age," said Pulcifer's father, "you couldn't pry me away from the television set. First thing in the morning. Last thing at night." Pulcifer's father sighed and shook his head. "I'd always hoped that my own son would follow in my footsteps."

"It isn't because we haven't set a good example," said Pulcifer's mother. "We're always watching television. And we've always had the nicest television sets. We've tried to make it easy for him. Color, remote control, even TV dinners."

"I just can't understand it," said Pulcifer's father.

4

Pulcifer's teacher couldn't understand it, either.

His class at school was divided into groups: the Eaglets, the Bluebirds, and the Sparrows. Pulcifer was the only one in his group, the Sparrows.

"I know you could be a Bluebird if you really tried," said Pulcifer's teacher, Mrs. Pruce. "Not that there's anything wrong with being a Sparrow, of course. We all start out being Sparrows. But look at Ethel Gawp. She used to be a Sparrow. Now she's a Bluebird. And the Bluebirds are already watching situation comedies and crime dramas."

Pulcifer couldn't seem to get beyond the cartoons and the commercials. And most of the time he didn't really understand those. He didn't get the point, that was it.

"You're not trying, Pulcifer," said Mrs. Pruce. "No one can teach you to watch television unless you try."

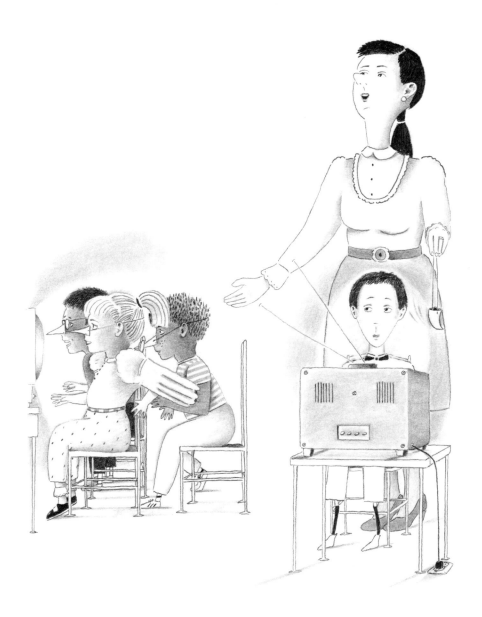

After school Pulcifer stopped at the library. There weren't too many books, because the audio-visual equipment took up so much room, but finally he found a book about a boy and his dog that he'd been wanting to read.

When he went to the desk to check it out, the librarian said, "It's very disappointing to see you taking out a book, Pulcifer, when you could be watching television. Do your parents know you come here to get books?"

Pulcifer shook his head.

"I didn't think so. I don't think they would like to know that you were coming in here, getting books out, taking them home to read."

She frowned at Pulcifer.

"I remember one boy, Pulcifer, who started with just one book. Two months later he was checking out three books. Three, Pulcifer! The habit had formed. It was too late to help him. What do you think of that?"

Pulcifer scratched his ear. "It's very interesting," he said.

When Pulcifer got home, he went to his room and settled down on his bed to read the library book. He had just come to the best part when his mother walked in.

"Oh, Pulcifer," she said sadly. "You're reading again." She sat down on his bed. "I just don't know where all this is going to end, Pulcifer. How are you ever going to learn to watch television if you spend so much time reading?"

After dinner that night Pulcifer's father said, "Your mother tells me you've been reading again, Pulcifer. Do you realize that you could have spent those same hours watching television, my boy? Now those hours are gone, gone forever. All those programs. All those game shows and soap operas and situation comedies and talk shows, gone, never to return."

Pulcifer's leg was going to sleep.

"It must be the school's fault," said Pulcifer's mother. "I'll have to have another talk with his t-e-a-c-h-e-r."

She called Mrs. Pruce.

"He simply can't keep up with the rest of the class," said Mrs. Pruce. "The other children watch a great deal of television. Some of our better students watch night and day."

"There must be something the school can do to help," said Pulcifer's mother.

"We can always try, of course," said Mrs. Pruce. "We'll put him in a special corrective remedial class for non-watchers."

The next day Pulcifer started attending the special class. His teacher was Mr. Plim.

"You can read all you want to," said Mr. Plim kindly. "Abiding by certain rules, of course. If we have no rules, we have no system, right?"

Pulcifer nodded. Then he shook his head. He wasn't quite sure what the right answer was.

"You don't have to watch any television at all while you're with us," said Mr. Plim. "We don't even have television here, so you can relax."

He pointed to a chair. "This is where you will do all your reading. We can't carry our books around any more than we can carry our television sets with us wherever we go."

Mr. Plim rubbed his hands together. "Now the first thing we'll do is select a book. You have several choices at this hour."

Pulcifer chose a mystery book, *The Case of the Mummified Mask.*

Mr. Plim looked at the big clock on the wall. "You've missed the first twenty-seven pages, but just plunge in at page twenty-eight and see if you can make any sense of it."

Pulcifer started to read. It took him a while to figure out the plot because he'd missed the first part, but it seemed pretty exciting:

> Joe felt his scalp prickle. He wheeled around. There, in a corner of the dark garden, a mysterious shape stood up.

Pulcifer turned the page. It was an advertisement. Mr. Plim looked over his shoulder. "We can't skip, you know. But there are only about ten pages of ads. Later, of course, as the book becomes more exciting, there will be more advertising pages."

Pulcifer started to read the advertisements:

> NEW! FOR THE FIRST TIME EVER!
> Self-heating TV dinners!
> Simply place on warm television set.
> "Your dinner will be ready when you are."

Finally Pulcifer finished reading the advertisements and could start reading the mystery again. He'd sort of forgotten where he left off.

> The shape drew nearer. Joe saw with relief that it was kindly old Mr. McGregor who lived next door.
>
> But what was that that he was holding? Joe stared. It was a gun. And it was pointed at Joe.

Pulcifer was pretty thirsty. Maybe he'd just go out to the bubbler in the hall to get a drink of water.

When he came back he picked up the book again.

"You missed the exciting part," said Mr. Plim. "I'm afraid you're just in time for more advertisements. And the ending. But we have other books scheduled for our next session."

When Pulcifer went to the special class the next time, Mr. Plim told him he could choose between two books. One was called *Mystery at Silver Creek* and the other was called *The Facts about Facts.*

Pulcifer chose *Mystery at Silver Creek.* After he had read a few pages, he found that it was a series of articles about the different kinds of vegetation that grew in and around Silver Creek, Nebraska.

He decided to read *The Facts about Facts* instead.

"I'm afraid you've already missed the first two chapters," said Mr. Plim.

Pulcifer started to read it anyway. It turned out to be a very exciting story about a time warp. It took him a while to understand it because he'd missed the first of it. Now he was just getting into the best part.

"Lunch time," announced Mr. Plim.

By the time Pulcifer had finished lunch it was too late to read *The Facts about Facts.* The other books that were available after lunch were very boring.

Pulcifer went to the special classes every day. At the end of a month, Mr. Plim had a conference with Pulcifer's mother.

"We've done everything in our power to turn Pulcifer against books," said Mr. Plim. "I'm afraid there's nothing more we can do."

Pulcifer's mother sighed. "Maybe I should take him to a p-y-s – a p-s-y: a psychiatrist," she said.

"A psychiatrist," said Pulcifer's father that evening. "Well, the best is none too good."

The next day Pulcifer's mother took him to a psychiatrist.

When they got to the office, the receptionist gave Pulcifer's mother a questionnaire to fill out.

Pulcifer looked over his mother's shoulder as she filled in the questionnaire.

Has the patient ever eaten nothing but raisins for more than three consecutive days?

Has the patient ever exhibited unusual interest in any of the following:

the color green
lamp shades
even numbers

Pulcifer stopped reading.

When his mother had finished filling in the questionnaire, the receptionist said to Pulcifer, "Dr.
Tawke will see you now."

Pulcifer followed her into the doctor's office.

The receptionist put Pulcifer's questionnaire on Dr. Tawke's desk and left the room. Dr. Tawke shuffled some papers around on his desk. Then he looked up at Pulcifer.

"Now, young man, we have to establish some rules, eh? Number one, you and I are friends. Don't think of me as your doctor, think of me as your pal."

Dr. Tawke reached over and shook Pulcifer's hand. Pulcifer wasn't absolutely positive but he thought that maybe two of his fingers were broken. He rubbed his hand. Maybe they were just sprained.

Dr. Tawke leaned back in his chair. "Mind if I call you Herbie?"

Pulcifer shook his head.

"Or perhaps you feel that Herbie is a baby name. Maybe you'd feel more comfortable with Herb."

Dr. Tawke pointed his finger at Pulcifer. "I want to make something absolutely clear, Herb. What we talk about will stay right in this office. You can tell me just what's bothering you and it won't go any further."

The only thing that Pulcifer could think of that was bothering him was that his fingers still hurt a lot.

Dr. Tawke leaned back and clasped his hands behind his head. "Would you be surprised, Herb, if I told you that yours is not an unusual problem? Let me tell you, Herb, there is nothing to be ashamed of. It is perfectly natural to be jealous of a new baby in the house. Perfectly natural."

He leaned forward. "I'm going to tell you something very, very interesting, Herb. I had problems adjusting to *my* baby brother when he was born! What do you think of that?

"I'm sorry to hear it," said Pulcifer. "I mean, I'm glad you told me, and it's very, very interesting, just the way you said it would be."

"Now, Herb, admitting our problems, facing up to them, is the first step in conquering them. You can tell me right out that you're jealous of the new baby and I'll understand."

"There isn't a new baby," said Pulcifer. "There's only me."

Dr. Tawke leafed through the papers on his desk once more. "Herbert Fishley," he said. "You're Herbert Fishley."

Pulcifer sighed. Maybe he *was* Herbert Fishley. It was sort of like trying to understand a program on television.

Dr. Tawke picked up another paper. "You're Pulcifer," he said. "Mind if I call you – um – Pulcifer?"

Pulcifer shook his head.

"Well, Pulcifer, I understand that you have a little problem. And the problem is that you haven't learned to watch television."

Dr. Tawke smiled. "I'm going to tell you something that will surprise you. I had exactly the same problem! Yes, Pulcifer, hard as it may seem to believe, I didn't know how to watch television. And yet I overcame my handicap, just as you can overcome yours."

He leaned forward. "You must strive, Pulcifer, you must struggle. You must buckle down and watch television as you have never watched before. Remember, there's no such word as can't."

That night Pulcifer's mother said, "I'm sure Dr. Tawke will get to the b-o-t-t-o-m of Pulcifer's p-r-o-b-l-e-m."

"It's our last hope," said Pulcifer's father.

Pulcifer went to Dr. Tawke's office many times. Every visit seemed very much like the visit before.

After a few weeks Dr. Tawke called Pulcifer's mother into his office. "I can sum up this lad's problem with one word. One word! And that word is *motivation.* It's as simple as that. Once he understands the reason to watch television, he'll be watching just like everyone else."

"Motivation," said Pulcifer's mother. "We never thought of that."

"My boy," said Pulcifer's father that evening, "we've solved your problem. Apparently you haven't understood the *reason* for watching television."

"Well, what is the reason?" asked Pulcifer.

"Everyone watches. There's your reason, son: everyone watches."

"I don't think it's a very good reason," said Pulcifer.

"But it's the only reason there *is,* dear," said Pulcifer's mother.

"I still don't think it's a very good reason," said Pulcifer.

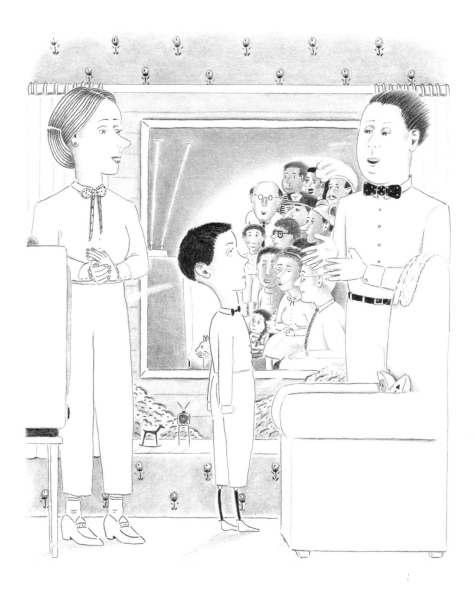

Pulcifer's mother sighed.

"We've done all we can," she said. "No one can say we haven't tried."

Pulcifer's father put his arm around Pulcifer's shoulder.

"We want you to know that we love you anyway," he said. "After all, a son is a son. We stand behind you, son."

"Yes, dear, even if you are d-i-f-f-e-r-e-n-t," said Pulcifer's mother, turning on the television set.

Pulcifer settled down comfortably with his new stack of library books.

DATE DUE			

FIC   Heide, Florence
HEI   Parry.

The problem with
Pulcifer.

LIBRARY MEDIA CENTER
VICTOR FALLS ELEMENTARY